MRS. DOG'S OWN HOUSE

story by Mary Calhoun

pictures by Janet McCaffery

Here is an inventive cumulative tale whose merry sense of fun masks a useful bit of wisdom: too much advice, however well-intentioned, can be a bad thing.

Mrs. Dog's house—a simple doghouse with soft blankets on the floor—seemed just right until her barnyard friends began to make suggestions. Mr. Rooster thought there should be a tower to watch the sun rise, Mr. Squirrel a staircase for scampering, Mr. Pig a kitchen, and so it went. Each time a friend thought of an improvement, Mrs. Dog hastened to carry it out, and each time her house grew more splendid. At last, when the building was finished, she had a grand mansion. And then, suddenly, Mrs. Dog realized her home was no longer a doghouse, no longer just right for her.

How Mrs. Dog solves the problem brings the story to a surprising and satisfying conclusion. With its gaily colored illustrations that expand upon the wealth of detail in the text, this picture book is one that will be asked for again and again.

MRS. DOG'S OWN HOUSE

story by Mary Calhoun
pictures by Janet McCaffery

WILLIAM MORROW & COMPANY | NEW YORK 1972

To Mike and his own Mrs. Dog, Cleo.

Mrs. Dog had her own house.
It was just big enough for her
to turn around three times and lie down.
Old blankets covered the floor.
The blankets were matted
with Mrs. Dog's hairs,
and they had a most satisfying smell.
Mrs. Dog liked her own house,
because it was the best house
in the world for a dog.

One day Mrs. Dog was lying in her house,
with her long nose over the doorsill,
when Mr. Rooster strolled by.
"Good morning, neighbor," said Mr. Rooster.
"All snug in your house, I see."
"Yes," said Mrs. Dog.
"It's the best house in the world."

Mr. Rooster scratched a little dirt
and eyed the house,
first with one eye,
then with the other eye.
"Well, not quite," he said. "Just barely.
It's not quite the best house in the world.
It doesn't have a tower, you know."

Mrs. Dog sat up.

She walked out of her house and looked at it.

"A tower?

Why does my house need a tower?" she asked.

Mr. Rooster flapped his wings.

"Why, you need a tower to watch

for the sun to come up," said Mr. Rooster.

"Anybody knows that!"

"Oh heavens!" Mrs. Dog exclaimed,

her whiskers getting all flustered.

"I never thought of that."

So Mrs. Dog got out her tools

and put on her carpenter's apron.

She gathered some boards and nails.

Also a tall ladder.

Mrs. Dog went to work

and built a tower on top of her house.

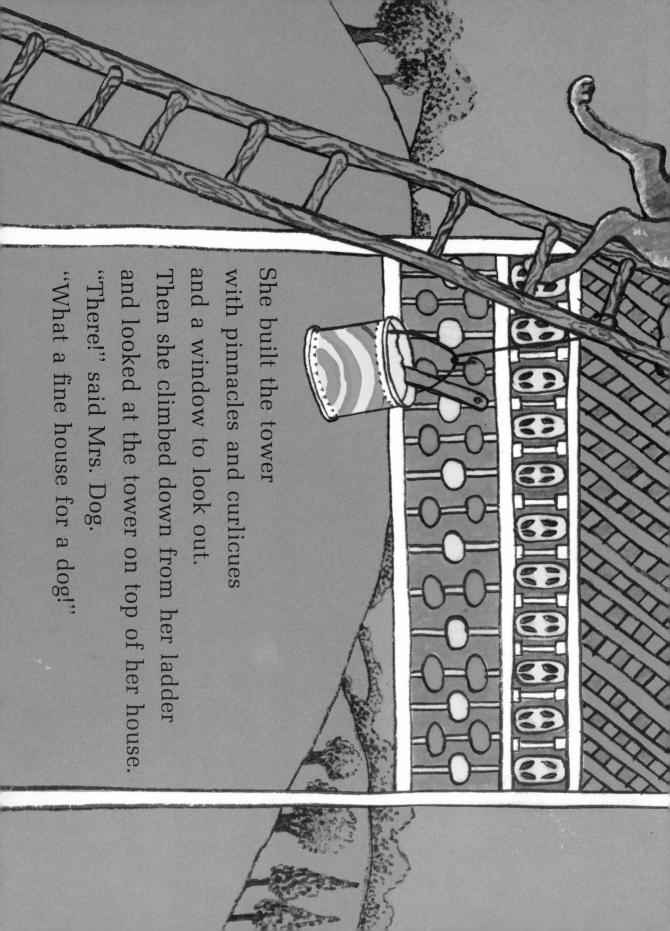

She built the tower
with pinnacles and curlicues
and a window to look out.
Then she climbed down from her ladder
and looked at the tower on top of her house.
"There!" said Mrs. Dog.
"What a fine house for a dog!"

While she was looking
and waving the plume of her tail,
Mr. Squirrel ran by.
"Nice house you've got there," said he.
Mrs. Dog invited him inside to see.
Mr. Squirrel scampered about,
trying to find something to jump onto.
"But how do you get
up to your tower?" he asked.
"What this house needs is a staircase.
And banisters.
Stairs to run up
and banisters to scamper along."
"Oh, of course," said Mrs. Dog.
"Why didn't I think of that?"

She got out her tools
and built a grand staircase
up to the tower.
She added banisters to go along the sides.
Last, she polished the banisters
with the corner of one of her blankets.
"There!" said Mrs. Dog.
"What a beautiful house for a dog!"

Mrs. Cat came pussyfooting along.
Mrs. Dog invited her in
to see the beautiful house.
Mrs. Cat looked at the staircase.
She sniffed at the blankets on the floor,
the blankets matted with Mrs. Dog's hairs
and strong with Mrs. Dog's smell.
Mrs. Cat turned up her nose.
"Well," Mrs. Cat said,
"it's all very nice, I suppose.
But if it were *my* house,
I'd have some pillows,
some lovely Turkish pillows to sleep on."
"How lovely!" said Mrs. Dog.
"Of course."
There wasn't room for a pillow corner,
so Mrs. Dog got out her tools again.

She built a nook onto her house
and filled it with pillows
in Turkish splendor.
"There!" said Mrs. Dog.
"Oh my, what a perfectly lovely house!"
But Mrs. Sheep came to call on Mrs. Dog.

She looked at the house.
And she only shrugged her woolly shoulders
at the Turkish-pillow corner
and the grand staircase
and the tower on the top.
"Oh, my dear," she said to Mrs. Dog.
"Your house is not nearly big enough.
You need a parlor to sit down in
when ladies come to visit."
"I forgot," said Mrs. Dog.
Her long nose drooped in shame.
Then she went to work with her tools
and added a parlor onto her house.
In the parlor she put a fireplace,
and over the fireplace
she put a marble mantelpiece,
and over the mantelpiece
she put a gilded mirror.

"There!" said Mrs. Dog.
"What a grand house for a dog!"
And what a fine lady she'd be,
in such a grand house!
Mrs. Dog smoothed her ears
in front of the mirror
and swished her tail
with its pure white plume.
Just then Mr. Pig came trotting over to see
what all the building and hammering was about.
Mrs. Dog invited him in
to see her grand house.
But Mr. Pig said, "Good gracious!
You don't have a kitchen.
How can you live in a house with no kitchen?
You need a banquet hall, too."
Mrs. Dog's ears flew up.
"Naturally," she said.
"I'm so glad you mentioned it."

She built on a kitchen
with a stone-paved floor.
She added a long corridor.
At the end,
she built a splendid oak-beamed banquet hall.
It even had wood-paneled walls.
Then when she was done building,
Mrs. Dog walked all around her house,
inside and out.
"What a mansion!" she cried.
"What a magnificent house for a dog!"

Mrs. Dog planned a banquet
in her magnificent house.
She hired a cook to prepare the food
and a proud-nosed butler to serve the food.
When all was ready,
she invited her friends to the feast.
They sat down in the banquet hall.
Around the table were
Mr. Rooster, Mr. Squirrel, Mrs. Cat,
Mrs. Sheep, and Mr. Pig.
At the head of the table sat Mrs. Dog,
waving the fine white plume of her tail.
"Let the feast begin!" she called.

j29193

In walked the proud-nosed butler,
into the banquet hall.
He carried a silver tray,
and on the tray were silver bowls.
The bowls were filled with raspberries.
Mrs. Dog looked at the tray.
She looked at the bowls
full of dewy red raspberries.
And she jumped down from her chair.

"Raspberries?" she cried. "Raspberries?
Dogs don't eat raspberries!"
"I do," said Mr. Pig, snuffing the tray.
"But I *don't*," said Mrs. Dog.
"And this is *my* house."
She looked at her house.
She saw the oak-beamed banquet hall.

She saw the grand staircase,

the marble mantelpiece,

the corner full of pillows
in Turkish splendor.

"Ridiculous!" cried Mrs. Dog.
"How ridiculous!"

Waving her tail, she banished the butler
and shooed out her friends.
She tore down the staircase,
tossed out the pillows,
knocked off the tower.
Mrs. Dog turned the mansion
back into her own house.
When she was done, she looked at it.

"There!" she said.
"That's the right house for a dog!"
Mrs. Dog went inside her own house,
turned around three times and curled up
on the blankets that smelled most satisfying.
"Whuff!" she said, tired and happy.
Then Mrs. Dog went to sleep
in the best house in the world for a dog.